The E...
Lighten-ing Conductor

This is Nicola's very first published book. She's been writing all her life (well nearly), but only decided to DO something with her stories when her children kept on asking what happened next!

Thousands of people hope to have their work published, so Nicola was staggered when Bloomsbury Children's Books chose her story!

Here it is.

She hopes you like it.
(She's writing another one now.)

NICOLA MATTHEWS

THE
EXTRAORDINARY
LIGHTEN-ING
CONDUCTOR

Pictures by Rachel Pearce

Bloomsbury

In memory of my father
Donald Matthews
who made the ordinary
extraordinary

First published in Great Britain in 1995
Bloomsbury Publishing Plc, 2 Soho Square, London, W1V 6HB

Copyright © Text by Nicola Matthews 1995
Copyright © Pictures by Rachael Pearce 1995

The moral right of the author has been asserted

A CIP catalogue record for this book is available
from the British Library

Pb ISBN 0 7475 2204 9
Hb ISBN 0 7475 2076 3

10987654321

Printed in Britain by Cox and Wyman Ltd, Reading, Berkshire

Chapter 1
UP, UP AND AWAY

IN AN ORDINARY street in an ordinary town, there lived an ordinary boy called Greg. He had ordinary mousy blond hair and ordinary blueish eyes. He wasn't especially tall, but he wasn't short either. He was quite clever and fairly bad at football but not absolutely terrible. Oh, and he was a bit of a worrier, but apart from that he was, well, ordinary.

He lived in an ordinary house with his

mum and his younger brother, Jack.

One morning Greg woke up to find that he was not as ordinary as he thought.

It happened like this. One ordinary Wednesday morning he was fast asleep in his bed when he should have been eating his breakfast. He was having a very strange dream about Mrs Marchpane, the dinner lady. She was waving at him as he flew over the school playground in his pyjamas. All his friends were playing in the yard, but no one but Mrs Marchpane saw him (which was just as well). She was calling out to him but he couldn't quite hear what she was saying.

Suddenly his mother's voice crashed through his dreams.

"Greg! Time to get up. Your porridge is getting cold!"

Nobody's mother had a louder voice than Greg's mother.

"You're a slow coach. I'm going to be first downstairs. Nanananana." Jack bounced out of the bottom bunk, grabbed at the corner of Greg's duvet and pulled it onto the floor. Nobody's brother was more annoying than Greg's brother.

Greg flopped one foot out of his bed and stood up. It was then that it happened. He banged his head on the ceiling. Something was wrong! He looked down. He was floating in midair! He grabbed the bed post to steady

himself. NO. He must still be dreaming. He must still be asleep, dreaming his strange dream. He closed his eyes tightly. When he opened them everything would be normal again. But when he opened his eyes he was still floating about a metre above the ground.

"Greg! You're late. I'm not telling you again. Get down here now."

What was he going to do? How could he get downstairs? Mum was bound to shout. Maybe if he could make himself heavier he'd be all right. He looked around wildly for something heavy. There – luckily he had hidden his favourite tank under his duvet so that Jack wouldn't find it. He grabbed it – it really was heavy.

"Take aim. Fire!" it said with an American accent.

It made Greg jump and he nearly dropped it.

"Take aim. Fire!" it said again.

"Greg. Are you playing up there?"

Mum had not just got the loudest voice of any mother he knew, but also the keenest hearing.

"No, Mum. Coming, Mum," he shouted back.

The tank seemed to do the trick. Holding it in one hand he quickly put his trainers on – they were heavy too – and made his way downstairs. That was very difficult. He sort of pulled himself down, clutching the banisters to keep from bobbing upwards like a helium balloon. How was he going to manage in school?

He was glad to get his legs under the kitchen table. He sat on a high stool so that his legs were wedged tightly against the underside of the table. It was very uncomfortable. At breakfast he managed to eat two bowls of stodgy porridge, three sausages, five slices of toast and two cups of tea. He felt sick but very heavy. Then he remembered it was

Wednesday – football with Mr Tafflin. Nobody had a games teacher as awful as Mr Tafflin. Oh, no! He started to feel even sicker.

"Mu-um. You said no toys at the table: Greg's got his tank," whined Jack.

Greg stuck his tongue out at him, and, checking his mother wasn't looking, kicked him under the table.

"Mu-um, Greg just kicked me."

"Don't tell tales, Jack. Greg, why have you got a tank at the table?"

"Er um ... It's for school ... A project ... We're doing transport and war and er ..."

"Oh, OK. Just go upstairs and get dressed. We're leaving in five minutes, dressed or not."

His mum was always cross in the morning – but there was just a chance she meant what she said. The thought of turning up at school in just his underpants was even worse than the thought of flying like a kite into the classroom. Somehow he would have to get dressed.

It was not very easy. He put gravel from his mother's potted plants into his pockets, and wore his thickest, heaviest and itchiest sweater. To make the job even harder, he tried to hang on to the tank while he was doing it.

"Come on, Greg, I'm desperate. Mu-um, Greg won't let me in the bathroom."

"Take aim. Fire!"

"Hurry up, Greg. What are you doing in there? I'm going. NOW."

Greg's big problem was going to be carrying the tank in school. He needed that tank. He had put it down for a second when he was alone in the bathroom. Then started to think about floating back up into the air and as soon as he thought about it, he did. He banged his head on the corner of the bathroom cabinet too. Why had this happened to

12

him? Nobody he knew could float above the ground like this. Ordinary people didn't just – well – fly.

"Come on, Greg!"

He'd got it – his rucksack, he could carry the tank in his rucksack. He grabbed the tank again somehow, found his rucksack, emptied his football kit onto Jack's bed (it was nice and smelly and it would serve him right). Then he put the tank inside the rucksack along with some wooden bricks and put it on his back. He didn't dare to think about what Mr Tafflin would say about his football kit – but what could he do?

"I'm going now!"

"Mum says we're going, Greg. You'll have to walk. Hahaha."

Feeling very heavy, very hot and very worried about Mr Tafflin, Greg ignored Jack and made it to the car. Could he pretend he'd got stomach-ache? His mum would never believe him – not after

13

he'd eaten all that disgusting porridge. All he could think about was what would happen if he started to float upwards, out of his seat in the middle of the classroom. He could feel himself blushing at the very thought.

To start with it wasn't too bad. Everybody was talking about the cartoon they'd watched before school. Everybody knew Greg never watched TV in the morning so nobody expected him to talk. He sat in his chair in his thick jumper and rucksack worrying quietly to himself. Then Lizzy noticed his jumper. His aunt, who worked for some animal charity, had given it to him. Not only was it heavy and itchy but it was deco- rated with several large pandas.

"Ooh, look – Greg's got a girl's jumper on."

"Isn't it sweet!" said Sasha. "And look, it's even got the panda's name on it

– Chi Chi!" She shrieked with laughter.

Greg felt himself get even hotter and even more uncomfortable and what was worse he couldn't think of anything to say.

Lizzy and Sasha, the prettiest and the naughtiest girls in the class, called him Chi Chi all morning and then Max and Harry started. Max was supposed to be his friend and Greg had been about to tell him about the flying. When Max started pulling faces at Greg and snuffling like a panda, Greg changed his mind. Greg hated to be laughed at. Then it was games with Mr Tafflin. Greg felt hotter still and even sicker than he had before. What was he going to do?

"Why aren't you changed into your games kit, Greg? Don't you want to take your lovely jumper off?"

Everybody giggled as if Mr Tafflin was the funniest man on earth.

Greg suddenly thought that flying

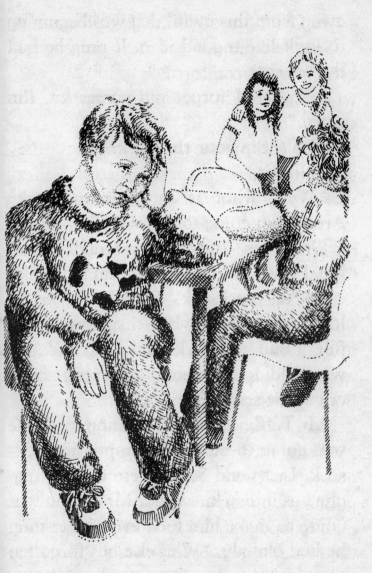

away from this awful day was beginning to look like a good idea. If only he had the courage.

"No, sir, I forgot my games kit. I'm sorry."

"Isn't it in your rucksack?"

"No, sir."

"Well, what is in your rucksack? Aren't you going to show us?"

Greg was getting hotter and hotter. No. Please don't let Mr Tafflin make him open his rucksack. Everybody would laugh even more when they saw it was full of building bricks and a toy tank. He was holding his breath and trying not to cry at the same time.

Mr Tafflin gave him a funny look. He was going to make him empty his rucksack. Lizzy and Sasha were already giggling as if they knew that Mr Tafflin was going to make him look even sillier than he had already. "Who else has forgotten their kit?"

A hand went up.

"Right. James, Greg, you come with me. You'll just have to use the spare kit I've just had given to me. And you can run twice round the field once you've changed."

Behind Mr Tafflin's back, James flashed him an evil grin. If Mr Tafflin wasn't about to find out what he was hiding in his rucksack, James would. James was easily the nastiest boy in the class, and probably the nastiest boy in the whole school. Greg began to panic again, but then Mr Tafflin said that James must get changed first while he had a word with Greg in private. Greg wasn't sure if that was good or bad.

"Greg, are you all right? You don't look very well." This really was the most extraordinary day ever – Mr Tafflin was being nice to him! That was almost stranger than waking up and finding he could fly.

"I'm feeling a bit hot and dizzy, sir, and my stomach hurts."

"Humm, well, get changed and if you feel ill when you're on the field, come and tell me. And don't forget your kit again."

James was already running round the field so the changing room would be empty.

Mr Tafflin handed him some baggy old shorts, a shirt and some really horrible looking boots. Somehow he now had to get changed and run round the field without flying away.

"Er, Mr Tafflin, sir, can I keep my rucksack on?"

"What?"

"Well, sir, my back hurts umm – I fell out of bed this morning and – erm it doesn't hurt so much if I keep my rucksack on."

Mr Tafflin was looking at him as if he was quite mad, but before he could say anything, Mrs Marchpane, the plump and friendly dinner lady, walked past. For some reason she winked at Greg and signalled to Mr Tafflin.

"Er – Excuse me, Mr Tafflin, can I have a word?" Mr Tafflin looked a bit surprised but walked over to talk to her. Greg wasn't sure whether he should go and get changed or not. Both Mrs Marchpane and Mr Tafflin glanced quickly in his direction and Greg had the feeling they were talking about him. When Mr Tafflin came back he gave Greg a rather strange look.

"Mrs Marchpane wants a word with you. When you've finished, I'd like you changed and on the field," he said, before walking off to stop the grass fight going on between Max and Eric.

"Hello, dearie," said Mrs Marchpane, looking at Greg's bulging pockets of gravel, his rucksack and thick, panda-decorated sweater. "You don't need all

that, dearie. Now, listen to me. When you're struck by lighten-ing you don't have to worry about a thing. It's a blessing, dearie, that's what it is. You worry too much. A boy your age shouldn't worry about anything."

Greg wasn't sure what to say. He hadn't been struck by lightning. There hadn't been a storm. What was Mrs Marchpane talking about?

"Now, dearie, don't look so puzzled. I know all about it. You've got a touch of the up, up and aways."

Did Mrs Marchpane know what had happened to him? How could she know?

"Now, dearie, I don't have time to show you now. And we'd both be a bit noticeable flying over the school, wouldn't we – but you've not got to worry. I would have explained it all in your dream, but you woke up before I had a chance. So listen carefully. If you want to fly, you have to think light, happy thoughts and if you want to come down, think sad, worried and heavy thoughts – you don't need all that clobber. You couldn't fly now if you wanted to – you're far too worried. Light thoughts to go up – thistledown and moths' wings, butterflies and kites, sunshine and breezes, oh, and lovely whipped cream."

As Greg watched in amazement Mrs Marchpane and her large shopping bag began to rise off the ground before his very eyes. She hovered, like a very large balloon in a raincoat, about thirty centimetres off the ground.

"Now you see, don't you, dearie? Trust me, I'm an expert. And to come down, you think heavy thoughts of lead weights and concrete, rhinos and buses, grey days and hailstorms, puddings and dumplings." As she spoke, Mrs Marchpane descended slowly and with great dignity back to the ground.

"Easy as anything. Don't you worry

about a thing, dearie. Now run along and do your best at football and I'll see you tonight." With a friendly wave she was gone.

Not knowing what to think on a day of such surprises, Greg quickly got changed and ran out onto the field. Mrs Marchpane was right. So long as he kept thinking worried thoughts and didn't think of flying, he stayed firmly on the ground. The only trouble was, it was very difficult not to think of something. As soon as you thought, "I mustn't think that," you'd already thought it. He was glad he was on his own because he did bob up off the ground a few times in the changing room. He kept repeating, "Lead weights and concrete, rhinos and buses," to himself, like a mad kind of shopping list.

Outside he didn't have a problem. He was so worried about flying away in front of his friends, he kept firmly to the ground. It was when he was playing football that he began to see that his new talent might turn out to be useful. The ball was coming for him – it was very

high. If I could just fly a little bit up in the air – he thought to himself, and before he knew what was going on, he was up in the air and heading the ball straight for the goal. He was so shocked to find his feet off the ground that he panicked and immediately fell back down and over onto the grass. But no one was watching him, the ball had gone in. He'd scored a goal just before the whistle blew.

Mr Tafflin said it was a brilliant header and it had won the match for the yellow team. Max said, "Well done!" And even James, who was not even on the same side, said "Good shot." No one made any more remarks about pandas for the rest of the day. Lizzy and Sasha gave him some crisps at lunchtime and for the first time ever he was picked first for football in the yard at afternoon break. He didn't score any more goals but he started to feel very happy. So happy, in fact, that he caught himself floating once or twice and had to murmur Mrs Marchpane's list to himself. Maybe being out of the ordinary was not going to be so bad after all.

Chapter 2
JACK FALLS DOWN

It wasn't until he got home that he remembered Mrs Marchpane saying something about seeing him later, or tonight, or something. He wondered what she had meant. What would his mother think if she turned up at his door? His mother had never met her. Would Mrs Marchpane tell his mother he could fly and what on earth would his mother say? She would surely tell him off about it. Everything else he did made his mother tell him off. He spent all evening worrying about Mrs Marchpane and his feet stayed firmly on the ground.

By bedtime, Mrs Marchpane still hadn't called and he began to relax. Perhaps if he waited until everyone was asleep he could try and really fly – in the dark when nobody could see. He hid his tracksuit bottoms and his hated itchy sweater at the foot of the bed along with his shoes, socks, hat and gloves. He was a sensible boy and he knew it would be cold flying in the middle of the night.

"Mu-um! Greg's put his kit in my bed and it's horrible and smelly and he's put his shoes on the bed, and they've got mud on them and you said…"

"Oh, shut up, can't you," snarled Greg. "Why do you always want to get me in trouble?"

"What are you arguing about now, you two? You should be grateful you've got a brother, not always fighting. Some people would be glad of a brother to play with."

"He's too young."

"I am not. Anyway, you're too stupid."

"I am not, anyway you're..."

"BE QUIET both of you. You are giving me a headache and if I hear another sound there will be BIG TROUBLE. Now good night." Mum kissed them both good night and tried to tuck them in. Jack's bed was so horribly smelly after Greg's games kit had been in it all day that she had to change the sheets. She gave Greg a very cross look, but didn't say anything. Greg saw her notice his muddy shoes on the bed and expected her to shout, but she didn't say anything. What was going on? Did she know?

"Sleep tight."

Greg didn't want to sleep. He wanted

to stay awake until everyone else was asleep. Unfortunately, Jack didn't want to go to sleep either. First of all he sang in a low voice all the songs Greg most hated. Then he lay on his back and started kicking the mattress above his head – Greg's mattress, where Greg's back was lying. Then, when even that didn't get Greg mad enough to hit him back, he started stealing all Greg's books and hiding them under his duvet. Greg was getting very angry but he knew that if he did anything at all, Jack would yell for Mum and he'd be in BIG TROUBLE. That was one thing about Mum, she always kept her promises – good and bad. At long last, even Jack got fed up with being annoying and fell asleep, but by this time Greg was asleep too.

He was woken suddenly by Jack shaking him.

"Greg, quick. Wake up! There's something horrible at the window. Greg,

Greg, ple-ase wake up. I'm scared."

Greg opened his eyes. It was dark and it was a minute before he could see anything, but he could hear very plainly. Someone was knocking at his window. Someone was outside.

"OK, Jack. It's all right. It's probably just a tree being blown by the wind."

"We haven't got a tree."

That was true. Greg looked about for a weapon.

"Pass me the cricket bat, Jack."

He slid out of bed, far too worried to fly. There was a face at the window. There was a hand tapping on the glass. Greg was shaking with fear. He clutched the cricket bat tightly. He made himself look at the face, trying to think what else it could be – a shadow perhaps, a mark on the glass and then he realised. It was Mrs Marchpane.

He started to float up off the ground with relief.

"It's all right, Jack. It's only Mrs Marchpane – you know, the nice dinner lady at school." Jack was looking at him in wonder.

"Greg – er – you're flying."

"Oh, yes, I am, aren't I?" He had never seen Jack lost for words before. Jack was staring at him as if his eyes were going to pop out of his head like a cartoon.

Smiling to himself at Jack's confusion, Greg floated gracefully across to the window and undid the catch.

"Hello, dearie. I'm sorry, I didn't know you shared a room with your brother. I think I gave him a bit of a fright. Are you ready then?"

"Ready for what?"

"Well, for a bit of flying practice, of course. I can't have you not knowing what you're doing and I don't want you flying around on your own at night. What would your mother think of me?"

"Mum doesn't know, does she?"

"No, of course not. Not that she'd mind, probably."

"But you don't know her!"

"Oh, don't I, dearie?" She smiled. "Well, never mind about that now. Get some woollies on – it's cold out here – that nice jumper you had on today would do fine."

"Oh, I'm sorry," said Greg, quickly remembering his manners. "Won't you please come in?"

He eyed the small window doubtfully. There was no way Mrs Marchpane would fit. He imagined his mum coming in the next morning to find a plump lady stuck halfway through his upstairs bedroom window. He started to sink to the floor again.

"Thank you, dearie, but I think I'm a little bit too well nourished for your bedroom window – and do stop worrying. Look at you, heavy as a rhino again. Let's go! Daylight will be here before we know it. Let's up, up and away!"

"I'm coming too." Greg had forgotten about Jack. "If you don't let me, I'll tell Mum. She said you were never to talk to strange ladies."

"Mrs Marchpane is not a stranger," said Greg hotly. But he had to admit she was quite strange, and although his mother had never told him not to go out flying at night with anyone without her permission, he had the funniest feeling that that was only because she had never thought of it. "Anyway, you can't fly."

"Now, boys, there is no need to argue," said Mrs Marchpane through the open window. "And you're making enough noise to wake the dead."

Seeing Greg's worried face she added quickly, "No, not really, Greg, dearie. It's just a saying. Now, Jack, get dressed up warmly and I'll give you a donkey ride but you'll have to hold on tight and BE QUICK!"

37

They were. Perhaps for the first time in his life Jack did what he was told first time and he didn't even whine. Carefully Greg lifted Jack out of the window onto Mrs Marchpane's back. Jack looked very frightened and very small. Greg

thought he was really quite brave because he didn't say anything. He just clung on very tightly to Mrs Marchpane's throat.

"No, not my throat, dearie, I can't breathe!" she said in a strained voice, and Greg held on to Jack while he put his arms round her shoulders. He was shaking. What if Jack were to fall? It would be his fault. Greg climbed onto the window ledge and made the big mistake of looking down. It was a very long way to fall.

"Come on, dearie," said Mrs Marchpane gently. She was hovering somehow just outside the window. Jack was looking at him in a worried sort of way. His eyes looked huge and scared in the light of the nearby street light. "You'll be fine – thistledown and moths' wings, butterflies and kites..."

"Sunshine and breezes," Greg muttered to himself. His voice sounded hoarse as if he hadn't used it for along time. He took a deep breath, shut his eyes and stepped off the window ledge into thin night air.

He did not fall. He hung suspended in the empty air outside his window. He could fly. He really could. Whoopeeeee!

"Well done, Greg! Now use your arms and legs as if you were swimming and let's go!!!!!"

It was easy. He had learned to swim a few years ago. He was best at breast stroke so he tried that. The air wasn't as still as he had thought and a light breeze played around his ankles. The night air made everything smell somehow stronger. He could smell the sweet, tangy flowers in next door's rockery. He could see over all the ordinary gardens of all the ordinary houses in his ordinary street and it was extraordinary, unbelievable, like magic. Maybe it was magic. Who cared? He could fly!.

Mrs Marchpane could fly fast for such a big woman. She was the most amazing sight. She looked so normal, as if she was just on the way to the shops, not speeding about the rooftops, shouting instructions on flying over her shoulder. Jack was still holding on tightly, but he was beginning to smile and Greg – Greg thought it was the most wonderful feeling ever. After a little while he started doing twists and turns in the air, just as if he was in water. The air held him up, like water in a pool.

There was hardly anyone about. A cat on the rooftops nearly fell off when it saw Greg fly by. A dog, sniffing by some rubbish bins, looked up, saw him and started to howl. He saw someone who looked like Mr Grunt, the caretaker,

riding his bicycle by the river, but Mr Grunt never looked up and he didn't see Greg. Once, as they flew through the centre of town, Greg thought he saw someone out of the corner of his eye who looked a lot like Mr Tafflin doing cart-wheels, high in the air over the railway station. But when he looked again, he had gone.

Some of the time he flew on his own, following Mrs Marchpane as she led the way and pointed out the sights. Some of the time he flew next to her and Jack, and just chatted.

"Mrs Marchpane, how has this hap-pened? Why can we do this? No one else can."

"Can't they, dearie?" she said inno-cently and she wouldn't tell him any-thing else.

"It's to do with my dream, isn't it? You made it happen through my dream, didn't you?"

But Mrs Marchpane just smiled and pointed out the Town Hall far below them.

They flew for a long time and Greg was beginning to feel tired. His arms were aching and his nose was cold. It was getting a little less dark all the time.

"Time to go back now, dearie, and catch a few hours' sleep before school. I don't want Jack falling asleep. Oh! er... No! Help!"

At that very moment, Jack had finally fallen asleep and his grip on Mrs Marchpane's shoulders had relaxed. Before she had time to catch him, he slipped and was falling, screaming down towards the town.

"Greg!" squealed Jack and Greg acted without thinking. He dived, his arms over his head, straight down towards Jack. He felt like an eagle with its wings pinned back, plummeting after its prey.

He could feel the cold air rushing past him as he hurtled down faster than he would have imagined possible, faster than Jack. He didn't think or scream or anything. He grabbed Jack by his jumper and held on. It was hard to keep his grip. Jack hadn't been lightened as he had. Jack was heavy but he mustn't let go.

"Mrs Marchpane! Help!" he panted. They were still falling downwards, though not so fast. He mustn't worry. He mustn't be afraid. He had to make them both fly now. He started to repeat under his breath, "Thistledown and moths' wings, butterflies and kites..." They weren't falling any more. Sobbing wildly, Jack grabbed Greg's legs with his arms. His grip was like a clamp.

"It's all right, Jack. I've got you safe. You're not going to fall."

He tried to make his voice calm and reassuring. Like his mother's voice the time he'd got his head stuck in the park railings. He didn't feel a bit calm. His heart was hammering inside his chest. Mrs Marchpane got there as he was about to panic. She arrived in a great fluster of skirts and raincoat.

"Oh, dearie, I just couldn't catch you. Are you all right? Here, let me take you." She picked Jack up in her arms. Even then, he wouldn't let go of Greg's legs. She talked to him gently and he let go. He still hadn't stopped sobbing. He was very frightened.

Greg suddenly felt very worried. What if he hadn't caught him? He couldn't even think about it.

"Come on, dearies. All's well that ends well. No harm's done and Jack's safe and sound and you were very brave and quick, Greg. I would have got to him before he reached the ground, I'm sure, but it would have been very close. Well done, Greg. Now Jack, dearie, I expect you want to go home."

The journey back didn't take long. Jack didn't say anything at all and Mrs Marchpane was unusually quiet. Greg was just pleased his brother hadn't hurt himself and he was quite pleased with himself too. Mrs Marchpane had said he was brave and quick. He wasn't brave really, he hadn't had time to think about anything brave but he had been pretty quick.

Greg got inside his bedroom first and Mrs Marchpane handed Jack over to him. He was still shaking a bit. He was quite a small boy really, much smaller than Greg imagined. It was hard to believe that such a small boy could be so annoying. He took him from her almost tenderly. Jack clung to him like a frightened baby.

"I've got him, Mrs Marchpane."

"Good night, boys, sleep well. See you tomorrow."

"Thank you!"

"Thank you, Mrs Marchpane," said Jack, in a small voice.

Greg put Jack down and shut the window.

"Are you all right now?" he asked.

Jack nodded and got into his bed.

"It was great – the flying, wasn't it?" said Greg.

"Yes," said Jack quietly. "Thank you for rescuing me."

"That's all right," said Greg casually. "You are my brother, after all."

Then no one said anything else as they both fell fast asleep for the second time that night.

Chapter 3
ALLY ON THE ROOF

"**B**OYS! Come on. It's five to!"

Greg rolled over. It was too early. He didn't want to get up.

Jack tumbled out of bed.

"Greg! Wake up! Was it real? Did it really happen?"

"What? Did what happen?" Greg was groggy with sleep. He flopped his legs over the side of the bed and stood up. He hit his head on the ceiling again. Jack looked at him.

49

"It's all true then? You did save me?"

Greg was rubbing his head and eyes and trying to think what he could have done to make his legs ache so much. He yawned.

"Boys! Get up!"

"Quick, Jack, grab my foot will you and pull me down. I'm too tired to think heavy thoughts."

Jack grabbed Greg's legs and tried to pull him down, but it was no good. Greg was as light as a balloon.

"Greg, wake up! Mum's coming! Quick."

"Lead weights and concrete, rhinos and buses..."

By the time Mum had made it up the stairs, Greg was firmly on the ground, inspecting his sore legs.

"Greg, wherever did you get those bruises?" His mother was standing at the door staring at his legs in horror. Greg looked blank.

"You got them playing football. Didn't you, Greg?" said Jack quickly. His mother looked at him in surprise.

"Well, I'll get some arnica cream. You should have told me about them, Greg. They look very nasty. Come on, we're late."

Mum seemed to be studying both boys very hard at breakfast. They ate in silence and they both looked very tired. Greg expected her to shout at them, but she didn't. She seemed less cross today, maybe because they weren't quarrelling.

As she washed up, Greg thought he heard her singing to herself. The words were very familiar. Surely she wasn't singing "Thistledown and moths' wings…" was she? He wondered why he wasn't worried that Jack might tell his mother what had happened. Jack was being very good. He could have told Mum when she had asked about his bruises, but he hadn't. Anyway, Greg

51

was too tired to worry about anything that morning, and he kept on having to repeat Mrs Marchpane's heavy list to keep himself from floating away in a daydream. Fortunately he started to worry about what might happen if he dozed off in school. Without his duvet to keep him down, would he float away while he slept? That thought kept him firmly anchored to the ground all morning.

It was a funny sort of morning in school. The roof was being mended and all morning the class was disturbed by the sounds of heavy footsteps on the class-room roof. There was scaffolding outside the window too, and Mrs Granger, his class teacher, warned everybody very firmly against playing on it. Even so, James and Eric dared each other to climb it at break time and got into big trouble.
    Unlike James and Eric, who spent

lunchtime in the head teacher's office, Greg had a very nice time. He was still a bit of a hero after his great goal the day before and once more he was one of the first to be chosen when Max and George, the star footballers, picked their teams for football. It was a nice feeling and he managed to score a goal without the help of his flying skills. He was very pleased by that, because although he was proud of yesterday's success, scoring a goal because he could fly felt a little bit like cheating.

The day was going very well until after lunch. Mrs Granger, who thought he was a sensible boy, sent Greg and Sasha to collect some junk for junk modelling from one of the infant classrooms. He didn't know why she had chosen Sasha because she wasn't at all sensible, but he never understood what went through the minds of adults. Sasha did a few hand-stands and cartwheeled across the playground – she was a terrible show-off. She laughed at his disapproving face and started to walk. Suddenly she pinched his arm, her eyes round with wonder.

"Look, Greg, LOOK – on the roof. Oh NO!"

Greg looked on the roof, and sitting right on the very edge of the roof was a small girl. She seemed quite happy. She was swinging her legs and singing to her teddy bear or some soft toy she was cradling in her arms. Sasha was about to call out, but Greg stopped her.

"No! Don't shout, you might frighten her and then she'll fall."

"But where are the workmen? There should be someone there. Where's her mum?"

"She must be from the nursery school next door and the workmen must be at lunch or something. Look, you go and run to the office and get help – call the fire brigade. I'll see if I can reach her. Run!"

As soon as Sasha had turned away, Greg ran as fast as he could to the scaffolding. In his panic he had forgotten that he could fly. When he got there he could see that part of the scaffolding had fallen away. What was he to do? There was a thud. Oh NO! She couldn't have fallen. There was a wail.

"Teddy..."

Greg raced round the side of the building. The little girl had dropped her teddy and was now looking down at the place where it had fallen. She suddenly looked very frightened.

Greg thought quickly. He ran forward, grabbed the teddy off the ground and, quickly checking that no one could see him from the windows of the school, began to mutter Mrs Marchpane's lightening words. It was hard because he was so worried that the little girl was going to fall. He forced himself to clear his mind. "Think light, happy thoughts," he told himself angrily. He remembered that moment the night before when he realised that he could really fly. He remembered his excitement.

He felt his feet rise slightly from the ground. He thought about the way he had turned and rolled with the cold night air in his face. He remembered how the town had looked far below him , how he had felt as if he ruled the world. He was getting higher. He wouldn't think about his brother falling or about that poor little girl. She had started to cry. Greg felt the earth beneath his feet again. This was no good – he had to do it. He had to fly or she would... "Come on. Stop worrying," he said aloud.

He thought of Mrs Marchpane flying with her raincoat flapping and he started to giggle. He thought about Jack being safe in Mrs Marchpane's arms after he'd rescued him. He'd managed to keep his head then. His feet began to lift again.

He began to feel noticeably lighter. "That's it, Greg. Fly," he muttered. He was away and beginning to reach the height of the school roof. He wasn't all that good at landing, so he just flew to where the little girl was sitting and began to hover there, like Mrs Marchpane had done outside his window. He must be careful not to startle her, but it was too late. The little girl had spotted her teddy in his hand and was leaning forward to grab it. She was going to fall.

Quick as lightning, Greg was there.

"It's all right, you can have your teddy now."

Greg caught her firmly by the arm to stop her falling. It was all right. She was still on the roof, but she had nearly fallen. Still holding the little girl's arm he managed to manoeuvre himself onto the roof. His feet weren't quite touching the surface but they were quite close. Very gently, he pulled her away from the edge.

"Now then. Here's your teddy. What's his name?"

"Teddy. Are you Superman?"

"Me? No. My name's Greg."

"I sink you're Superman. You can fly. Mummy says real people doesn't fly. You're not real. Are you a cartoon?"

"No, of course not," said Greg. This was not turning out quite as he had expected. Little girls weren't supposed to be so nosy. Shouldn't she be crying for her mummy or something? Not asking him difficult questions.

"What's your name?" he said, in the voice he'd heard grown-ups use to small children.

"Not telling you," she said shortly.

"What are you doing up here?"

"Nuffink."

"Where's your mummy?"

"I've runned off."

"How did you get up here? Did you climb?"

The little girl shook her head. She had bobbles keeping her hair in pigtails and they rattled as she moved. Greg wondered how old she was. Three and a half, four maybe. It was hard to tell. She wasn't very tall. She must have been a good climber to climb that scaffolding. He wouldn't have liked to do it.

"You must be a good climber."

She smiled. "I'm brilliant. I'm going to be a mountingeer when I've growed up, but the climbing fame broked." She pulled a face. "I nearly felled, but I

59

holded on very tight. Wasn't I clever?"

"You were very clever," said Greg and he meant it. She smiled again. At last he'd said something right.

"You come and sit here with me and in a minute a big fire engine will come and rescue you. You'd like that, wouldn't you?"

The little girl nodded. "You can call me Ally."

Just at that moment, a very flustered woman came running out of the nursery school followed by two of the nursery teachers. She was screaming.

"Alice, Ally. Where are you? Darling, come back! Ally! Ally!"

"It's all right. She's here with me," called Greg at the top of his voice. Thanks to his difficult conversation with Ally he was pleased to notice that his feet were now resting firmly on the school roof. He felt quite heavy and rather sorry for the harassed looking woman who was probably Ally's mother. He'd thought Jack was naughty!

The woman looked around, searching for the voice.

"We're here on the roof. She's quite safe."

When the woman saw Greg perched on the roof, her daughter in his arms, she fainted right away. It was at that moment that the situation really got out of hand. A large red fire engine roared up the road, its lights flashing and its siren

blaring. All the firemen leapt out, wearing full fire-fighting gear, including gas masks.

Following behind the fire engine was an ambulance also with its lights flashing and sirens blaring. At least they could help Ally's poor mother. Behind the fire engine and the ambulance was a TV van, two newspaper journalists with cameras and a local television crew. At the same time, Sasha emerged from the school office with the head teacher, Mrs Wigglemore, Mr Tafflin the games teacher and Miss Hardacre the school nurse. Greg began to get worried. A small crowd of passers-by was beginning to gather outside the school, the builders were returning from their lunch break and Max, his friend from his class, wandered into the playground looking for him. He saw Greg and waved.

"What are you doing up there? You're

in big trouble when Mrs Granger finds
you. We've been waiting for the junk to
do junk modelling for ages. Who's that
with you?"

He looked a bit crestfallen when Mr
Tafflin came up to him. Greg couldn't
hear everything he said but it was clear
that Max was being told off for being
noisy. Greg just caught the words "disturbing the whole school". With all the
noise from the ambulance, the fire engine
and all the other people milling around
the school, Greg thought it was a bit
unfair to accuse Max of disturbing
everybody.

Greg waved back at him cheerfully
and shrugged very obviously, to show
Max that he thought Mr Tafflin was
being a bit unfair too.

It didn't take long for the firemen to
back the engine into the playground and
get the ladders up to the school roof.
One fireman started to try and climb the

scaffolding but soon saw that it had broken. In moments, the rescue was under way and Ally was safe in the arms of a burly fireman. She was not in the least worried. Greg just heard her say, "I like your hat. Can I have one?" And then it was his turn. As he came down the ladder everybody cheered and the firemen clapped. He was so embarrassed, he knew he had blushed bright red.

That was not the end of it. The ambulance men insisted on checking him over and making sure he was not suffering from shock. Then, as if she couldn't trust a man to do a thorough job, Miss Hardacre had another look just to make sure. Ally's mother hugged him and promised him anything money could buy for rescuing her dear, darling, naughty daughter. Then Miss Wigglemore came to talk to him and tell him that while he had been very brave, she hoped he wasn't going to make a habit of climbing dangerous scaffolding. She had had to give a severe telling off to two boys already that day for being silly. Scaffolding was VERY DANGEROUS. Then it was the turn of the newspaper men. They wanted to take a picture of Greg with Ally on his knee.

"Tell me," said one, with bad breath and dandruff on his coat, "how did you climb past the broken bit of scaffolding?"

"He didn't climb, silly, he flied," said Ally.

Greg began to wish he hadn't rescued her. Fortunately the newspaper man thought she was joking. He laughed.

"Well...er um," began Greg, doubtfully. Luckily Mr Tafflin saw him struggling and took control of the situation.

"I'm terribly sorry, Mr er...but this young man has been through a very distressing experience. I'm afraid the school can't allow him to be interviewed. Oh, dear me, no. I'm sure Greg's mother wouldn't want him to be bothered like this. I knew you would understand."

As he spoke, he swept Ally off Greg's knee, presented her back to her mother with a smile and ushered Greg away from Mr Dandruff or whatever he was really called. Greg was beginning to like Mr Tafflin. He squeezed Greg's shoulder reassuringly and whispered, "Your mother's on her way to take you home."

"You called her at work!" Greg was horrified.

"Don't worry, Greg. She isn't cross. She said she's very proud of you, but she always knew you were brave and she'll be here any minute."

"Mum said that!"

"Yes. Don't look so surprised. She's very understanding, your mother."

Greg was about to say that he'd never noticed. Then he suddenly thought – how did Mr Tafflin know his mother

was understanding? He didn't like to ask.

The funny thing was that when his mother arrived she *was* very understanding. She smiled and said, "Well done," and gave him a hug. She didn't even ask him a single awkward question. She took him out for a pizza as a treat – just the two of them. Mum laughed and made jokes as she hadn't for ages. Greg laughed too and a couple of times found himself beginning to bob out of his seat. Laughing made him lighten almost immediately. Fortunately the restaurant was empty and Mum didn't seem to notice.

After the pizza, which was Greg's favourite, they shared the most enormous ice cream he had ever seen, let alone eaten. Very happy, very full and very pleased with himself, Greg and his mother went off to collect Jack from school. It had been one of the most exciting days he had ever had.

Chapter 4
THE ALMOST CRASH

THE NEXT DAY the papers were full of Greg's heroic rescue – there was even a bit on the local news. Greg felt very uncomfortable about it. He hadn't really been brave. He hadn't climbed the broken scaffolding. He had just flown.

Mum took the next day off work and kept Greg and Jack at home. Jack had a temperature and Greg had a sore throat after his night-flying adventure.

Normally Mum would have made Greg go to school, but she thought it was a good idea for him to stay off school until he was quite well and until the fuss had died down.

After lunch Mrs Marchpane called to see him. This time she knocked at the front door in broad daylight. Luckily, her feet were firmly on the ground – it was the first thing Greg checked. She brought him some grapes. He expected his mum to be surprised, but when Mum saw Mrs Marchpane she got very excited and gave Mrs Marchpane a hug, as if she'd known her for years. Then she rushed off to make her a cup of tea. When Mrs Marchpane and Greg were alone she whispered, "Well done," to him.

"But I wasn't brave, was I?" Greg said, fighting back tears.

"Of course you were, dearie, there's more than one kind of courage. You risked being found out and I know you didn't want that. You put the little girl first and, most importantly, you conquered yourself."

"What do you mean?"

"Well, you were worried and you managed to forget that, so that you could fly. That's a very hard thing to do. You did well, dearie, and you shouldn't be ashamed of all the fuss."

Mrs Marchpane didn't stay long, but she promised to see Greg soon. She winked at him as she left, so he guessed she meant that they would go out flying again.

After she'd gone, Mum, Jack and Greg sat around eating chocolate and grapes, playing games and reading stories. Mum didn't have to rush about shopping or cleaning or washing, and nobody shouted or argued for the whole day. It was brilliant.

It didn't last. The whole of the next

week, Greg was teased and called the "local hero". He got quite fed up with it. Most people did seem to think more of him because of his rescue and Sasha and Lizzy both asked him to tea. It was Max, his best friend, who caused him the most trouble – going on and on about it. If it had not been for Mrs Marchpane's nightly flying lessons Greg might have been miserable. Instead, he was just very tired. Mrs Marchpane still wouldn't answer any of his questions.

Two weeks after that, everything was pretty well back to normal. He played with more children in his class than he had before. James, who had been awful to him for years, decided he was all right and he got a regular place in the lunchtime football games. Things were better with Jack too, though he wouldn't go flying again, no matter how hard Greg tried to persuade him.

The biggest problem was that Greg

was really getting tired. Mrs Marchpane was still taking him flying most nights, just for a few hours. It was great. They had explored the area for miles around. They had rescued three trapped cats, found one lost dog and a bicycle, replaced the weather vane that had fallen off the church spire and Greg had learned to fly upside down. Even so, some nights all he wanted to do was sleep.

One Wednesday night, about a month after he first discovered he could fly, Greg decided that he really must tell Mrs Marchpane that he needed a rest.

As usual, Jack heard her knocking and woke Greg up.

"Greg, Mrs Marchpane's here. She's been waiting ages. Hurry up! She says it will be dawn soon if you don't get moving." He was holding Greg's outdoor clothes and yawning.

Greg struggled out of bed and Jack helped him on with his jumper. "Thanks, Jack, I'll see you later."

"Have a nice time. Be careful you don't fall. 'Bye, Mrs Marchpane, 'night, Greg."

He was back in bed and snoring before Greg had even got out of the window. Jack was getting tired too.

Mrs Marchpane and Greg flew side by side in silence. Greg wasn't quite awake, though the cold air was waking him up pretty quickly.

"Where shall we go tonight, dearie?"

"I don't know, Mrs Marchpane – you choose."

"I fancy following the railway track over to Tarbridge and seeing the lake by moonlight. OK by you, dearie?"

"Great, Mrs Marchpane."

"Now, Greg, there's something I've got to tell you. Your time is nearly up."

"What do you mean, Mrs Marchpane?"

She nudged him gently in the right direction.

"Oh, look! Mrs Braine's left her buggy out again. It's going to get very wet. Looks like rain tonight. Just nip down and close it up for her, dearie, and put it under the porch. Such a scatterbrain!"

Greg did as he was told. He knew how to do it because Mrs Braine had left her baby buggy out every day for a week. He did wonder who she thought put it away for her every night – elves?

In a few minutes he was back, flying over the rooftops towards the open countryside. What was Mrs Marchpane talking about?

They flew on a bit further, Mrs Marchpane pointing out a family of foxes playing in the field below.

"What did you mean just now, Mrs Marchpane? What did you mean when you said that my time was almost up?"

"Oh, dearie, I do so hate this bit. I'm afraid this is our last bit of up, up and away-ing. You see you've been able to fly for a month now and that's about as much lightening as I can manage. But because it's your last night, I'll answer your questions…well, if I can anyway. You do see, dearie, all good things come to an end – this flying thing – it isn't for ever."

Greg didn't know what to say. He hadn't thought about it really. He'd got used to being able to fly. He didn't want to give it up.

"So, you did make it happen," he said, at last. "You did do it, in my funny dream – like I thought."

"Yes, dearie, your mother christened me the 'Extraordinary Lighten-ing Conductor'," she laughed uproariously. "You know. Because I wave in your dreams like Mrs Price, who conducts the

school choir, and make everyone light –
very witty your mother."

But Greg wasn't laughing – he didn't
really get the joke.

"My mother?"

"Why yes, dearie. She was my very
first, what would you call it? My very
first flying friend. Years ago now – she
was about your age. She was first and
then... I think it was Ted Tafflin."

Mr Tafflin and his mother! So his
mother had known all the time. Why
hadn't she said anything?

"Of course, it's a big secret – I make
everybody promise not to tell. What
would the papers say if they got hold of
it? Oh, good gracious me no – that
would never do."

Greg couldn't quite take this in. His
mother had once been able to fly! And so
had Mr Tafflin! He remembered suddenly thinking he had seen Mr Tafflin
turning cartwheels over the station.

"Can Mr Tafflin still fly?"

"Well…er yes, I rather think he can."

"But you said that it wasn't for ever, so how can he?" He was struck by a sudden thought. "Mum can't still fly, can she?"

"No, no, your mother had her month years ago. Mr Tafflin – well, dearie, he's never quite got the hang of it. He's never managed to – what's the expression? 'Lighten up.' He's never grown up, that boy."

Greg tried to think of Mr Tafflin as a boy – and failed. They flew for a while in silence while Greg tried to understand what he'd been told. At last he asked her.

"Mrs Marchpane, are you a witch?" At this, she roared with laughter until her eyes watered and her flying got rather wobbly.

"Oh, dearie, I wish I had a pound for every time someone has asked me that question. No, I'm not a witch – more of a fly-by-night." She guffawed again loudly, though Greg couldn't really see the joke.

"But you want to know how I came to be able to lighten people. Is that right, dearie?"

Greg nodded. He couldn't imagine what she was going to say.

"Well, it was a kind of miracle, really. One Sunday afternoon I was struck by lightning and after that I was struck by lighten-ing and I've been flying ever since. Every few years or so I dream of a child I know, wave to them and find I've made them lighter too – for a while anyway. Oh, my goodness! Look down there!"

Greg looked where Mrs Marchpane was pointing. They were flying over the railway track, which was a single track branch line. As they looked, two trains were powering towards each other from opposite directions. Greg could see their lights quite clearly in the darkness.

"Quick! You take that one. I'll take this one. Fly low in front of the driver! MAKE THEM STOP!" Mrs Marchpane cried. And she was gone, diving for the nearer train her skirts flapping wildly over her thermal long johns.

Greg had further to fly. He fought his rising panic and swam – flew – as fast as he could. The train was nearer. It was time to dive. What if he couldn't get out of the way of the train in time? What if he started to get worried at just the

wrong moment and fell in front of the train? He just wouldn't. That was all.

He raised his arms above his head like a diver just as he had done to rescue Jack and began to fall, faster and faster, towards the approaching train. The train was going very fast indeed. It was going to be hard to get in front of it. Think, Greg! He counted the seconds it took to go the short distance between telegraph posts. "One potato, two potato, three..." That wouldn't give him long enough. What could he do?

Don't panic! He would fly to a spot some way ahead of the train and start flying across the track when it was three telegraph poles away. That should give him enough time to flit in front of the driver's window. Then he remembered. He was wearing dark clothes so he wouldn't be seen. He'd seen a film once where children had waved red petticoats to stop a train. He wasn't sure what a petticoat was, but he did have a white hanky. He pulled it out of his tracksuit bottoms – it was clean. He flew down low, no more than a metre and a half off the ground and waited, treading air like a dog treads water. Six telegraph poles, five, four, three. Now! Using all his speed, he concentrated on flying in front of the train, just in front of the driver's window.

He caught a glimpse of a man's startled face and half flew, half threw himself out of the path of the train. There was a terrible screaming and screeching of brakes and a choking stench of brake fluid and diesel. The engine made a sound like a dying animal and ground to a halt.

Greg hid in the bushes, panting in shock. He was trembling all over but the train had stopped! He could not hear the other train coming, so Mrs Marchpane must have managed to stop her train too. Where was she?

He was a bit too nervous to fly off and find her. The train driver had climbed out of his cabin to see what was going on. Greg could see now the other train was no more than fifteen metres away. The driver's face looked very pale and shocked in the brightness of the headlights. He signalled at the other driver and the two men walked towards each other, angry and scared.

Greg slipped away on foot to find Mrs Marchpane. It was easier to walk. He suddenly felt very frightened. He had only just got across the line in time. What if Mrs Marchpane had acted first and then had not been able to think later? What if she had not left enough time to get out of the way? He could hear the men talking in low voices by the track. He caught the words "White bird", and "signal failure". The two men seemed quite dazed; he supposed they knew that they were lucky to be alive.

But what of Mrs Marchpane?

"Psst. Greg. Over here. I'm stuck." It took a moment for Greg to work out where the sound was coming from, but Mrs Marchpane was all right. She could still talk anyway.

"Up here!"

He looked up and there was Mrs Marchpane, wedged between two branches of a tall tree. Her raincoat was all tangled and torn, her long johns were in shreds and her face and hair were full of twigs and leaves. She was beaming and waving her arms.

"Great job, dearie, we did it!"

It was quite a job to get Mrs Marchpane out of that tree. Greg tried pushing and he tried pulling, but it was useless. It didn't help that both of them were giggling hysterically the whole time. Mrs Marchpane looked a sight, but Greg was so pleased to see her, he wanted to hug her – only a million sharp branches were in the way. In the end it was the laughter that did it. Mrs Marchpane had a great laugh, even when she was trying to laugh silently. Her whole body jiggled and wobbled with mirth and it was all a bit much for the tree. The branch gave way with a terrible tearing, splitting sound and she was free.

"What was that?"

The two men still talking on the track, stopped to listen. They moved a bit closer together, and then one of them went to get a torch.

"Quick! fly as fast as you can behind those trees," said Mrs Marchpane. "If we keep low they won't see us. We can get some height again when we're out of their sight."

"Mrs Marchpane, are you all right?"

"Fine, thanks, dearie, but if I were a cat I'd have lost another of my nine lives tonight," and she laughed.

"Since Mum knows all about you,

won't you come home and have some tea? Mum says it's good for shock."

"Well, do you know, Greg, dearie, I rather think I will. I haven't had such a close shave – well – for years."

Greg's mum was amazingly cool for someone woken in the middle of the night by her son, who was supposed to be in bed, and a rather battered looking old lady. She made Mrs Marchpane hot, sweet tea, wrapped her in a blanket and tended her cuts and bruises. She made up a bed for her in the spare room and didn't ask a question until Mrs Marchpane and Greg were both clean and warm and comfortable in front of the fire.

When Mrs Marchpane had told her the story, and Greg had added his bits, Mum looked pretty shaky herself. She poured some brandy in their tea – for medicinal purposes.

"Dear Mrs Marchpane, I'm very pleased for Greg that you've given him this chance to fly, but I must say I am very relieved Greg's month is over and I can start to sleep at nights. You really do attract trouble like a magnet. You have not changed a bit!"

"Thank you, dearie, but you have. You've forgotten the lightening words for too long, you know. Even though they won't make you fly any more, they will make you, now what's that modern expression, lighten up. I never knew such a pair of worriers – and young Jack's the same. I think you could do with a few changes in this house, a bit more thistle-down and moths' wings, butterflies and kites. Night night, dearies, and don't forget now – lighten up!" And with that Mrs Marchpane propelled her huge bulk lightly through the air and up to bed.

"Why didn't you tell me, Mum?" asked Greg, when she had gone.

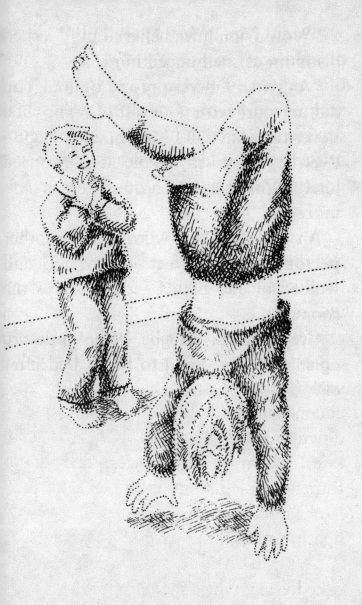

"Would you have believed me?" asked his mum as she hugged him.

"Anyway, I'm very proud of you. You did far more with your gift of flying than I ever did. And Mrs Marchpane's right – I've been too miserable and worried lately. What we need around here is a bit more fun."

And, without any warning, his mother performed a perfect cartwheel and walked on her hands – right across the room.

Greg smiled. Maybe being ordinary again was not going to be so bad after all.

Hope you enjoyed the story, folks! Now watch Greg fly you back through the pages by flicking the pages with your thumb.

I wish I could fly like that!

See how much you know about flying –

turn the page for some uplifting flying facts...

Spaced out!

What was the name of
the Russian dog who
was launched into
space in 1957?

A giant leap for Dogkind

Bumbling along!

What was the most famous musical piece composed by Rimsky-Korsakov in 1900?

Bee careful!

If you were running from a wasp and a bumble bee, only one of them, on average, would be fast enough to catch you. Which one?

Yikes!

BZZZZ